CLEMENTINE
AND THE
BEST
SLEEPOVER

ISBN 978-1-63630-021-4 (Paperback)
ISBN 978-1-63630-022-1 (Digital)

Covenant Books, Inc.
11661 Hwy 707
Murrells Inlet, SC 29576
www.covenantbooks.com

CLEMENTINE AND THE BEST SLEEPOVER

Taliah Hall

Clementine's birthday just passed. Her mom and dad were having a birthday party for her and invited Clementine's grandparents, aunts, and uncles. She had never had a sleepover before, and her parents figured since they were having a birthday party for her, why not do a sleepover, too? They told Clementine she could invite four girls to spend the night. Excitedly, she invited two of her cousins, Grace and Amber, and her two best friends, Charlotte and Bella.

Clementine was extremely excited and could not wait for the big day. Clementine and her mom made a list of everything they would need for the party. The next day, they went shopping for everything on that list. Her mom even let her pick out a few of her favorite candies and drinks. Later when they got home, they started making spaghetti and meatballs; that is Clementine's favorite meal.

5

Clementine offered to do the decorating. Blowing up balloons is Clementine's favorite part of decorating. Clementine was so busy decorating and helping her mom that she did not even realize what time it was. Before she knew it, her guests were arriving.

7

After they ate, she brought her friends outside to play on her trampoline. All her friends started jumping and played a game to see who could jump the highest. Jumping on the trampoline made them all extremely hot. So they ran and jumped into the pool where they played fun water games like Marco Polo and water tag.

As they were drying off from the pool, Clementine's mom came out and said, "Girls, would you like to do some crafts and have some snacks?"

While eating snacks, some of the girls painted pictures, and others made their own craft. Clementine's mom walked into the room with a big colorful cake that she had made for Clementine. Her family and friends started singing happy birthday to her. She made a wish and, then with one big blow, blew all the candles out.

Everyone was still eating cake when her parents brought in her gifts. Clementine opened all her presents; she got a doll, jump rope, basketball, Bible, and lots of new clothes. Her favorite gift of all though was the electric scooter her parents bought for her.

It had started to get late, and people were beginning to leave. Once they left, all the girls got ready for bed. Then before bed, they played some board games and had snacks.

15

Clementine's mom came in the room after about an hour and said, "It's time for bed, girls."

They said their good night prayers and went to bed.
When they woke up, they all got dressed and made the beds. Walking down the stairs, they all smelled something good.

19

In the kitchen, Clementine's mom had prepared pancakes, bacon, and fruit for the girls.

After enjoying a delicious breakfast, they went outside to play hopscotch and ride Clementine's new electric scooter.

Within a little time, all her friends were picked up by their parents.

Clementine had a blast and wished she could do sleepovers all the time.

The End

"I will give thanks to You, for I am fearfully and wonderfully made; Wonderful are Your works, And my soul knows it very well" (Psalms 139:14).

ABOUT THE AUTHOR

Taliah Hall is fifteen years old. Other than being an author, Taliah enjoys being with her family and friends. She also enjoys being outside and playing basketball. When she has free time, Taliah plays with her Bernedoodle, Theodore. She is from a little town in Rhode Island. Some of the profits from her book will be going to outreaches in her local communities.

CPSIA information can be obtained
at www.ICGtesting.com
Printed in the USA
BVHW020222271021
620013BV00016B/793